THIS  BOOK
BELONGS TO

_____

Which Eurps are in your first name?
Your middle name?
Your last name?
Can you name them all?

THE ALPHABET

EURPS™

VISIT SCHOOL

The EURPS were conceived and created by Barbara Harris

Produced by Arvid Knudsen

Written by Liane Onish

Designed by Kent Salisbury

Background art by Ann Wilson

EURPSVILLE USA INC.
MANHASSET NEW YORK

Ace Eurp asked Bipple,
"What will we do in **SCHOOL**?"
Bipple said, "Lots of fun things!"

*Find the letter sticker that is missing
from the sign and put it in the picture.*

In school we LISTEN...

"Listening! Eurps love to hear stories!" exclaimed Ace.
He used his Eurp magic and Sammy, Tom,
Omar, Roy, and Yolanda appeared.
"Shh," said Sammy. "Let's listen!"
Ms. Wendy read a funny **STORY**.
Bipple and the Eurps laughed.

Find a pillow sticker for Bipple and put it in the picture.
Then touch the Eurps that spell STORY.

...and SPELL...

"Spelling! Eurps love **WORDS**!" exclaimed Ace.
He used his Eurp magic and Wally, Omar, Roy, Dean,
and Sammy appeared. Then Harry, Benny, and Cece
joined them.

"Let's rhyme!" cried Roy.
The Eurps helped Bipple spell words that rhyme with AT.

Find the sticker of the cat Bipple drew and put it
on the chalkboard. Then touch the Eurps that spell WORDS.

...and READ...

"Reading! Eurps love books!" exclaimed Ace.
He used his Eurp magic and Benny, two Omars,
and Katie appeared.
"Books!" cried Benny. "Let's read a **BOOK**!"
Bipple and the Eurps sat in the library and read.

Find a book sticker for Benny and put it in the picture.
Then touch the Eurps that spell BOOK.

...and WRITE...

"Writing! Eurps love to **PRINT**!" exclaimed Ace.
Ace used his Eurp magic and Peter, Roy, Iris, Nellie,
and Tom appeared.
"Let's write a story!" cried Peter.
The Eurps sat at Bipple's table and wrote stories.
Bipple drew a picture for his story.

*Find a pencil sticker for Bipple
and put it in the picture. Then touch
the Eurps that spell PRINT.*

...and EAT...

"Lunch! Eurps love **FOOD**!" exclaimed Ace. Ace used
his Eurp magic and Fiona, two Omars, and Dean appeared.
"Let's eat!" cried Fiona.
Bipple opened his lunch box. Ace took a piece of apple.
Fiona ate half a sandwich. The two Omars took carrot sticks,
and Dean opened Bipple's thermos.

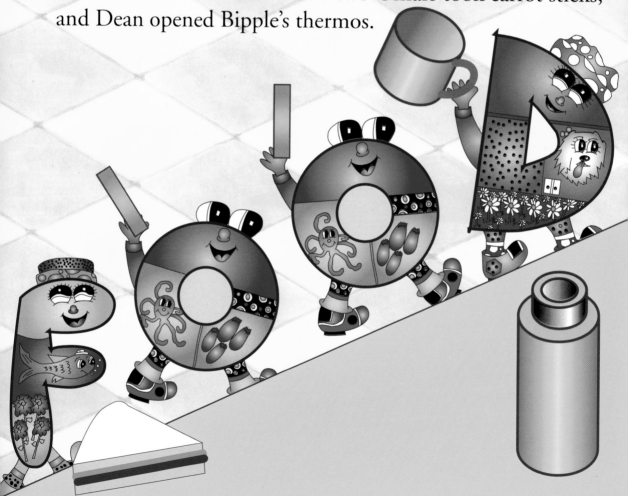

Find a sandwich sticker for Bipple and put it in the picture.
Then touch the Eurps that spell FOOD.

"Arithmetic! Eurps love **MATH**!" exclaimed Ace.
He used his Eurp magic and Mikey, Tom, and Harry appeared.
"Let's count!" cried Mikey.
Bipple wrote the number 5 and put 5 blocks next to the number.
He wrote the number 6 and put 6 toy cars next to it.
What number goes with the shells?

Find the missing number sticker and put it in the picture.
Then touch the Eurps that spell MATH.

...and SWING and CLIMB and SLIDE...

"Recess! Eurps love to **PLAY** on swings and slides
and jungle gyms!" exclaimed Ace.
He used his Eurp magic and Peter, Lizzy, and Yolanda appeared.
Bipple and Peter had fun on the swings.
Lizzy and Ace climbed the jungle gym. Yolanda liked to slide.

Find the sliding Eurp sticker and put it in the picture.
Then touch the Eurps that spell PLAY.

…and PLAY…

"Free time! Eurps love puzzles and **GAMES**!"
exclaimed Ace. He used his Eurp magic
and Gail, Mikey, Enid, and Sammy appeared.
"Games!" cried Gail. "Let's play!"
Bipple did a jigsaw puzzle.
The Eurps played a board game.

Find the missing puzzle piece sticker and put it in the picture. Then touch the Eurps that spell GAMES.

…until it is time to go HOME.

"**SCHOOL** is great!" exclaimed Ace Eurp.
"What did you like best?" Bipple asked.
Ace said, "I liked it all! When can we go again?"
"Tomorrow," said Bipple.
"Hooray!" cried Ace, Gail, Sammy, Benny,
Wally, Mikey, Lizzy, and Peter.

*What did Lizzy like best? Find the sticker
and put it in the picture.
Then touch the Eurps that spell SCHOOL.*

HIDE AND SEEK

Sammy, Cece, Harry, Omar, Omar and Lizzy have hidden the letters
S, C, H, O, O, and L in Bipple's classroom.
Can you help Bipple find the letters?
Circle each letter you find.
Then write SCHOOL on the line below.

___ ___ ___ ___ ___ ___

RHYME TIME

The Eurps want to help you spell words that rhyme with AT and IT.
Write in the missing letter for each word.

The AT Word Family

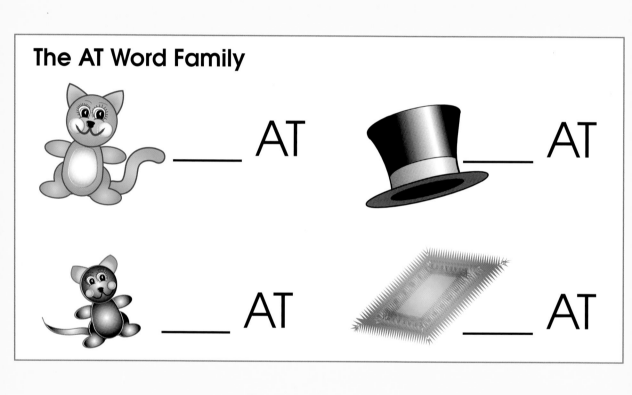

_____ AT

_____ AT

_____ AT

_____ AT

The IT Word Family

___ IT

___ IT

___ IT

___ IT

Close your eyes
and put your finger on an Eurp.
Then name things that begin
with the same letter.